MUFFINS FOR MUMMIES

Adam & Charlotte Guillain • Lee Wildish

DEAN

A boy called George heard mysterious tales
About the museum at night.
The cakes in the café had **vanished away**,
But the **cake thief** was nowhere in sight.

"Trixie," said George, "there's a case to be solved.

We *can't* dilly-dally or wait."

He packed up his bag with the gear he would need,

And took **twenty-five muffins** as bait.

Inside the museum, strange shadows loomed large

And eerie sounds echoed around.

"Look, Trixie," George whispered, "the thief must be near –
There are **cake crumbs all over the ground!**"

George held up a muffin to tempt out the thief,

And he called, "I've got cakes for a feast!"

But a deafening noise made him tremble and turn

And in thundered . . .

. . . a huge
woolly beast!

"A mammoth?" said George. Could *he* be the !

"He's going to charge at us – yikes!"

They ran through a doorway to make their €

And stumbled upon . . .

. . . some old bikes!

George hopped on a saddle and pedalled like mad.

The mammoth let out a great ROAR!

"He's going to catch us!" George panted in fear,

But the mammoth . . .

. . . got stuck in the door!

"Aha!" shouted George. "He's too big to get in,
So he *couldn't* have stolen the cakes!"
But, in all of the rush, he had not stopped to check
If his bike had a **bell** or some **brakes** . . .

CRASH! went the bicycle, CLASH! went the shields
As a Roman display tumbled down.
Then George saw a figure with **crumbs at his feet.**
"You're the cake thief!" he cried with a frown.

GRUMPICUS

"A cake thief?" The Roman glared down in a rage.
He really looked very upset.

"Help, Trixie!" cried George, as he darted and jumped
To escape from the Roman's **huge net**.

George leapt in a chariot, quick as a flash,
And his dog pulled him out of harm's way.
The Roman **tripped up** on his net with a howl,

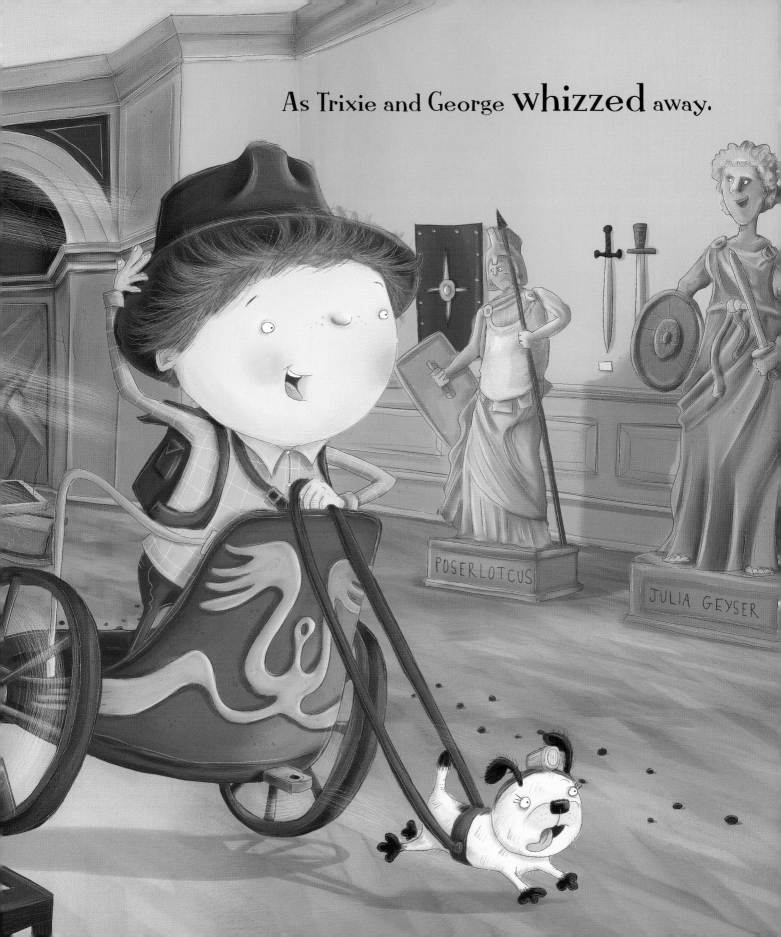

As Trixie and George **whizzed** away.

POSERLOTCUS

JULIA GEYSER

They swerved and they zigzagged and slid to a stop.

"We're safe!" George exclaimed in relief.

Then he spotted more crumbs in a trail on the floor.

"Look, Trixie! Now, let's **catch the thief!**"

George held out a muffin. "Is anyone there?"

He glimpsed something in the dim light.

He heard a loud clanking as someone drew near –

And then out of the gloom stepped . . .

. . . a knight!

"So YOU are the thief!" said George. "Where are the cakes?"

The knight **raised his sword** with a cry.

"How dare you accuse me?" he bellowed. "A *thief*?"

"Quick, Trixie!" George shouted. "Let's fly!"

The daring detectives began their escape,
There were weapons and shields everywhere.
George sprang in a **catapult**, threw his **lasso** –
And then . . .

They shot off through the air!

George fell with a bump in a dark, chilly room.

He switched on his torch to explore.

"Ancient Egypt!" he gasped. "Trixie, don't be afraid!"

Then he spotted **more crumbs** on the floor.

"Quick, follow that trail! We can still catch the thief!"
But Trixie had started to shake.
A **sarcophagus** stood with its lid open wide,
And inside was . . .

...a **huge** pile of cake!

George jumped as a voice bellowed,

" Look! There he is!
That boy stole the cakes - I was right!"

The **mammoth** and **Roman** were blocking the door,
And towards him was marching the **knight!**

"Admit you're the thief!" said the knight with a growl.

Poor George backed away, shouting, "No!"

Then he pointed his finger and whispered, "What's that?"

From the shadows a voice called . . .

"Hide!" shrieked the Roman and, "Help!" yelled the knight.
"Don't be scared!" said the **mummy**. "I'm nice!
It's my birthday today and my party starts now,
I've got plenty of cake – **have a slice!**"

"So YOU stole the cakes," murmured George with a gasp.

"And stealing is bad!" said the knight.

"But I can't have a **party without any cake!**"

Wailed the mummy. "That wouldn't be right!"

George opened his bag and they all peered inside.

"Have these **muffins!**" he said with a grin.

"We can take back the cakes to the café and then . . .

... the party can really begin!"

To our mummies, Rita and Chris xx
A&C Guillain

DEAN

First published in Great Britain 2017 by Egmont UK Limited
This edition published 2019 by Dean,
an imprint of Egmont UK Limited,
The Yellow Building, 1 Nicholas Road, London W11 4AN

www.egmont.co.uk

Text copyright © Adam and Charlotte Guillain 2017
Illustrations copyright © Lee Wildish 2017

The moral rights of the authors and illustrator have been asserted.

ISBN 978 0 6035 7770 3
70753/001
Printed in Malaysia